# LEROUX
## GOES TO
## NANA'S

### SAM WYLIE

ILLUSTRATED BY HAYLEE ALBRIGHT

Quantity sales special discounts are available on quantity purchases by corporations, associations, and others. For details, contact the publisher at the address above.

Orders by U.S. trade bookstores and wholesalers. Email info@BeyondPublishing.net

The Beyond Publishing Speakers Bureau can bring authors to your live event. For more information or to book an event contact the Beyond Publishing Speakers Bureau speak@BeyondPublishing.net

The Author can be reached directly at BeyondPublishing.net

Manufactured and printed in the United States of America distributed globally by BeyondPublishing.net

**BEYOND**
PUBLISHING

New York | Los Angeles | London | Sydney

ISBN: 978-1-637921-21-0

# DEDICATION:

I would like to dedicate this book to Leroux whom I miss so much. My grandma Paula Shook ( aka Nana) who always encouraged everything I wanted to do and try, I know she would be proud of this book. Dr Banovic, Dr Austel, Sam and Tiara along with the rest of the staff at UGA dermatology who went above and beyond for us, I am beyond grateful for all of you. Also the amazing internet family in Official Bulldogs Are Awesome Club who helped me have an extra year with my special girl.

"Come on Leroux it's time to wake up, we have to pack so you can go stay at nana's while I'm gone." Leroux just kept snoring peacefully on her bed, ignoring me as usual. "Come on Leroux, if you get up and help me pack I will give you a Cheeto!"

Leroux came flying off her bed and into the kitchen, impatiently waiting for her promised Cheeto.

"Alright, Leroux you get one Cheeto now and more when we finish packing for Nana's."

Leroux runs to her toy bin to grab her favorite rainbow unicorn, her bone, and squeaky ball. Once she makes sure those are placed in her suitcase she grabs her food bowl, the second most important thing she's taking to her nana's. What's the most important item to pack? Food!

Leroux watches me closely as I scoop her food into a bag. I know she's making sure I put in extra, she likes to make her nana think she didn't feed her and usually gets an extra meal out of her. Of course, I cannot forget the Cheeto's.

"Okay Leroux, let's load up and go to nana's!"

Leroux prances to the car and does circles in excitement waiting at the car door to be lifted into the seat.

" UGH Leroux, you're getting too big for me to lift you in. This is why the vet calls you big bootie Judy."

Now that we are loaded up and Leroux has her window down we can cruise to Nana's. Leroux has her head hanging out the window, slobber flying out of her mouth. I am obnoxiously singing " to grandmother's house we go" to her over and over until we pull in the driveway.

Nana is out on her porch waving as I open Leroux's door. Leroux goes flying out and tackles her Nana with excitement.

"Leroux you need to let Nana get up. You didn't even notice she had a present waiting for you on the porch swing."

Leroux quickly spots her new donut toy and starts squeaking it as loud as she can.

After all the excitement Leroux needs a nap so she goes inside to the couch to snuggle with her nana. Leroux's snores put her nana to sleep.

Leroux wakes up and decides she needs a snack and since nana is sleeping she will get her own treat from her bag, she knows mom packed her Cheetos.

Leroux bites, tugs, and rips the bag open. It's like Christmas, a whole bag of Cheetos and nobody there to tell her no!

Leroux ate the whole bag of Cheetos! Her face and feet were stained orange! Leroux thought, "oh no I better get this mess off so Nana doesn't know who made the mess on the rug". She trots up to the bedroom and hops in the bed, "what a perfect place to rub and scoot the Cheeto dust off my face and paws" she thought.

Leroux hears her Nana yelling downstairs " who made this mess"?

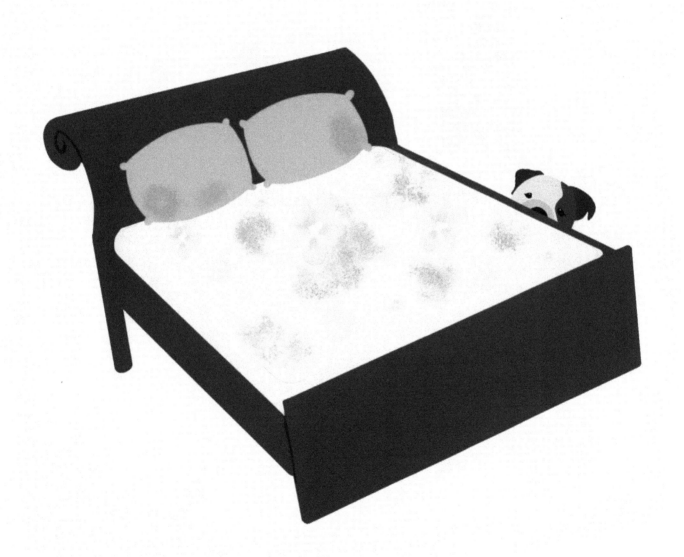

Thinking she's in the clear, she goes downstairs and sits by the mess while it is cleaned up and smiles at her nana. Leroux forgot, she has Cheetos stuck in her teeth! Nana promptly said " Leroux, did you make this mess? And don't lie to me because I see the evidence stuck in your teeth".

Nana cleaned the mess up and Leroux apologized by giving her many kisses. Once Nana accepted the apology she took Leroux outside to help her plant flowers.

"Leroux! Don't sniff the flower with the bee it's going to sting you"! She quickly jumps back and moves on to another flower to smell, this time one that doesn't have a bee on it.

"Leroux, are you eating your Nana's flowers"? With a mouth full of flowers Leroux looks at Nana and spits the flowers out. Leroux thought since they smelled so good she would just try one bite!

After they are done watering the flowers, Nana tells Leroux " it's time to come inside now and we will have some dinner".

Leroux got so happy she took off running down the hill in the backyard, tripped over her feet, and rolled into a mud puddle. Leroux doesn't miss a beat though, she continues running into the house covered in mud so she can have dinner.

"Leroux!! Nooooooo" Nana screams and she sees her clean kitchen get mud flung all over it. Leroux looks innocently at her food bowl hoping this doesn't delay her dinner time. Nana can't be mad at her cute squishy face so let's her eat dinner before bathing her. Leroux is chowing down as if she didn't just eat a whole bag of Cheetos a few hours before. Nana wiped up the kitchen and took Leroux for a bath.

"There, now you are all clean. Please don't make any more messes before your mom comes to get you". The night goes on and Leroux plays with toys, gets belly rubs, and cuddles on the couch with her Nana. Now it is time for bed. Nana tells Leroux " come on let go to bed now, you can sleep with me but no snoring or farting".

Leroux stops to get a drink first as her Nana heads upstairs for bed. Then a sudden scream from the bedroom, " Leroux what did you do to my sheets?! They are orange"! Leroux had forgotten she rubbed off the Cheeto dust in the bed earlier.

They get the sheets changed and head to bed, Nana hoping the rest of Leroux's stay is not nearly as eventful as the first day.

Leroux is sound asleep snoring and dreaming about having donuts for breakfast.

The next few days at Nana's are a breeze. Leroux was on her best behavior and even helped pack her bag to come back home. Nana said, " Leroux your mom will be pulling in any minute"! Leroux rushed to the front door and put her feet up on it looking out for her mom.

I pulled into the drive to see the cutest squishy face pushing against the screen door waiting for me. Once I got out of the car Nana opened the door and Leroux came flying out to greet me. " I know, I missed you too," I told Leroux over and over between all her kisses and hugs. I asked, " did you behave yourself for Nana this weekend"?  Leroux looked at Nana and Nana replied " what happened at Nana's stays at Nana's."

# SPONSORSHIP PAGE

Deborah Dahl Ross

Pam and Ron Noe

Jim and Barbra Wylie

Doug Smith

Gayla Hudson

Johanna Gemmill

Kenyon Smith

Lyndsey Hunt

Barb Howe

Misty Montoya Taylor

Grady and Samantha Norris

Kym Cool

In memory of Browning & Benelli

In memory of Abbey- Alyson Hovila Fleury

CPSIA information can be obtained
at www.ICGtesting.com
Printed in the USA
LVHW071205290921
699023LV00002B/5